Snap! Snap!

Colin and Jacqui Hawkins

MAMMOTH

It began with a snap, snap, snapping.

Out from under Sally's bed came a great hairy green
monster.

"Just what I need for my supper!" said the monster.

He grabbed Sally, tucked her under his arm, and carried her off into the night.

In the hairy, scary darkness there were other monsters, all fighting and squabbling.

When they saw Sally the monsters stopped fighting.

They all wanted to eat her up for their supper.

But Sally was not going to be anybody's supper.

She hit one of the monsters on the nose with her teddy bear.

She was very cross. The monsters cried and said they were sorry.

"If you're very good," she told them, "I will play with you."

The monsters jumped up and down with excitement.

"Let's go to the playground!" they shouted.

First they played on the see-saw.

Then they all fell off.

Next they ran to the slide, pushing and shoving to get to the top.

Down they went one after the other, over and over again.

When they were tired of the slide, they rushed off to
the swings. "Me first," said Sally.

The monsters put her·on the swing and began to push.

Sally swung higher and higher.

Then the rope snapped and she flew out into the night, leaving the monsters behind her.

Sally twisted and tumbled through the darkness.

She was falling, falling, falling, down, down, down . . .

. . . and landed back in bed with a bump and a thump.

First published in Great Britain 1984
by William Heinemann Ltd
Published 1996 by Mammoth
an imprint of Reed International Books Ltd
Michelin House, 81 Fulham Road, London SW3 6RB
and Auckland, Melbourne, Singapore and Toronto

10 9 8 7 6 5 4 3 2

ISBN 0 7497 2766 7

A CIP catalogue record for this title
is available from the British Library

Printed in Hong Kong
by Wing King Tong